The Horse
Must Go On!

A SUMATRA STORY

By Sibley Miller

Illustrated by Tara Larsen Chang and Jo Gershman

Feiwel and Friends

For Julie, Rachel, Lindsey, and Lacey—Sibley Miller

For Tory, who knows just what this dedication means
—Tara Larsen Chang

For Susan Summit Cyr, for her artistic talent,
endless patience, and enthusiasm
for all things equine—Jo Gershman

A FEIWEL AND FRIENDS BOOK
An Imprint of Macmillan

Printed in China. Printed in November 2009 in China by Leo Paper,
Heshan City, Guangdong Province.
For information, address Feiwel and Friends,
175 Fifth Avenue, New York, N.Y. 10010.

Library of Congress Cataloging-in-Publication Data
Miller, Sibley.
The horse must go on! : a Sumatra story / by Sibley Miller.
p. cm. — (Wind Dancers ; #3)
Summary: After seeing their human friend, Leanna, practice for a school
talent show, Sumatra decides the tiny, winged horses should put on a
show of their own, but finding their talents proves to be difficult.
ISBN-13: 978-0-312-38282-7
[1. Magic—Fiction. 2. Horses—Fiction. 3. Talent shows—Fiction.] I. Title.
PZ7.M63373Hom 2008   [E]—dc22   2008012788

DESIGNED BY BARBARA GRZESLO
Feiwel and Friends logo designed by Filomena Tuosto

First Edition: 2008

3 5 7 9 10 8 6 4

www.feiwelandfriends.com

CONTENTS

Meet the Wind Dancers

One day, a lonely little girl named Leanna blows on a doozy of a dandelion. To her delight and surprise, four tiny horses spring from the puff of the dandelion seeds!

Four tiny horses with shiny manes and shimmery wings. Four magical horses who can fly!

Dancing on the wind, surrounded by magic halos, they are the Wind Dancers.

The leader of the quartet is **Kona**. She has a violet-black coat and a vivid purple mane, and she flies inside a halo of magical flowers.

Brisa is as pretty as a tropical sunset with her coral-pink color and blond mane and tail.

Magical jewels make up Brisa's halo, and she likes to admire her gems (and herself) every time she looks in a mirror.

Sumatra is silvery blue with sea-green wings. Much like the ocean, she can shift from calm to stormy in a hurry! Her magical halo is made up of ribbons, which flutter and dance as she flies.

The fourth Wind Dancer is—surprise!—a colt. His name is Sirocco. He's a fiery gold, and he likes to go-go-go. Everywhere he goes, his magical halo of butterflies goes, too.

The tiny, flying horses live together in the dandelion meadow in a lovely house carved out of the trunk of an apple tree. Every day, Leanna wishes she'll see the magical little horses again. (She's sure they're nearby, but she doesn't know they're invisible to people.) And, the Wind Dancers get ready for their next adventure.

CHAPTER 1

All That Jazz

"And a-ONE, a-TWO, a-ONE, TWO, THREE, FOUR!" Sumatra tapped out a dancing beat, kicking her front legs and shouting at the top of her lungs.

Kona, Sirocco, and Brisa, who were flying alongside their fellow filly, stopped to hover in the air and *stare.*

Not only was Sumatra marking her moves, she was dancing. In mid-air! As she spun around and around, the shimmery ribbons in her halo spun, too.

"Um, Sumatra?" Kona asked gently.

"*What* are you doing?"

"Huh?" Sumatra asked absent-mindedly. Then she kicked her hind legs up, did another spin, and murmured, "And *two*, two, three, four."

"Hello!" Sirocco said. He flew over to Sumatra and grabbed the end of her pretty pale-green tail with his teeth, stopping her in mid-spin. "We're *supposed* to be looking for a new adventure this morning. Not spinning around like a dizzy bird!"

Sumatra blinked at her friends.

"Oh, right," she said. "Sorry, guys. I guess I just got caught up in it."

"In *what*?" Brisa asked, looking confused.

Sumatra's eyes gleamed as she pointed toward the ground with her nose.

"In *that*!"

She was gazing down at the sprawling lawn outside the school in the little town not far from the dandelion meadow where the Wind Dancers lived. Children were playing kickball, swinging from a jungle gym, and jumping around a hopscotch court. But it was a group at the edge of the lawn that had caught Sumatra's eye.

Six girls were swishing their hips from side to side. Their ponytails swung from side to side, too!

"They look like horses with those tails!" Brisa said admiringly.

"They really do," Sumatra replied with a giggle. Then she noticed one ponytail in particular—a pretty, wavy blond one. With a start, she realized that it belonged to—

"Leanna!" Sumatra cried. "Look, you guys! That's our girl! And she's the *best* dancer."

Kona, Brisa, and Sirocco gasped as they recognized their friend.

"Smile," Leanna was saying to the other girls. "And don't forget your jazz hands!"

The girls grinned widely, bumped each other's hips, and threw out their hands, fanning their fingers.

"See!" Sumatra said to her friends. "*That's* what got me going."

She did another light spin and then added dramatically, "Their dancing spoke to me. I was powerless to stop myself."

Sirocco rolled his eyes.

"Well, *you* may be powerless, but *I'm* not," he said to Sumatra. "Next time you feel the need to go flailing around in the sky like a

wet butterfly, just let me know. *I'll* help you
stop yourself."

Sumatra pouted.

"Hey," she complained. "If you can't say
anything nice, don't say anything at all!"

"All right, then," Sirocco replied with a

mischievous grin. "It would sure be *nice* to get going soon and go find our next adventure!"

"But, Sirocco," Brisa said, looking down at the dancing girls, "Leanna and her friends *are* pretty entertaining."

When the girls finished, red cheeked and breathless, the flying horses (well, all of them except Sirocco) whinnied their approval.

"That was amazing!" Sumatra breathed.

Leanna seemed to think so, too.

"Well," she said to her group with a firm nod, "it looks like we all know our parts for the school talent show. Should we practice again tomorrow?"

The girls responded with a chorus of mock groans.

"Hey," Leanna scolded them (with a smile). "You want to be fabulous in the show, don't you?"

"Of course we do, Leanna!" said one of

the girls. "We'll be there."

"With blisters on," joked another girl.

"Blisters?" Brisa chirped from up above
the girls. "Maybe they
should go to the black-
smith and get some
new shoes. That's what
the big horses in the
paddock do when *their*
feet hurt."

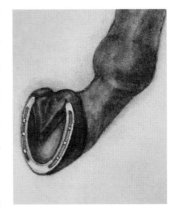

"Um, I think that's
just a horse thing,"
Kona corrected her. And then—

Brrrrriiiiingggg!

The bell rang.

The Wind Dancers watched wistfully as
Leanna and her friends made their way into
school.

"Oh," Brisa said with a sigh, "I wish they
could have seen us cheering for them!"

"Uh-huh," Sumatra said, her brown eyes shining. "I'm *most* impressed with Leanna. She was the director of the whole number."

"You're right," Kona agreed proudly. "She's a born leader."

Thoughtfully, the Wind Dancers rose higher in the air and began to fly toward their tree house.

"So!" Sirocco said. "What should we do next? A picnic? Some swimming in the creek?"

"How about a nap?" Brisa suggested with a big yawn.

"What?" Sumatra said. She was gazing at Brisa, her mouth hanging open. "How can you think about napping? How can you think about *anything* but that amazing dance number? The hip waggling. The *jazz hands*! It was the most amazing thing I've ever seen!"

Sirocco looked blankly at Sumatra for a moment—before turning to Brisa.

"You know, I *am* kind of sleepy, too," he said. "Maybe we *should* take naps."

Sumatra stomped her hoof (or would have, if she'd been standing on the ground).

"I'm not tired at all," she protested.

Now, it was Kona who yawned.

"We did get up super-early this morning," she said, nodding understandingly at Brisa and Sirocco.

Sumatra felt desperate.

"I've got an idea," she blurted. "An idea for an adventure like no other!"

This got her friends' attention.

"What is it?" Brisa asked breathlessly.

"Yes," Kona asked with wide eyes. "Where do you want to go?"

"The question," Sumatra said slyly, "is not

where. It's *what*! And *what* I think we should do is put on our *own* talent show, for all our animal friends around the dandelion meadow, just like Leanna's doing!"

"*What* do you mean?!" Sirocco balked. He stopped in mid-air and gaped at Sumatra.

"You don't want us to dance, do you?" Kona added, looking uncomfortable.

Brisa looked down at her legs. "Is it even possible to do jazz hooves?"

"Listen," Sumatra said. She hoped she sounded as confident as Leanna had been with her friends. "All we need to put on a show is a director like Leanna. And *I* can do that job."

"That's great, Sumatra," Kona said gently. "But doesn't a talent show require, you know, *talent*?"

"Yeah," Brisa said uneasily. She patted her glossy blond mane. "If this was a beauty

pageant, I'd have no worries. But I don't know what my talents are."

"Neither do I," Sumatra said. "But I know how to find out! Don't worry, guys. You go take your naps and leave everything to me!"

CHAPTER 2
American Bridle

A few hours later, after Kona, Brisa, and Sirocco woke from their naps, they stumbled out of their sleeping stalls. They stretched and yawned their way into the kitchen.

"I don't know about you two," Kona said, running a hoof through her tousled mane, "but that was the best nap I ever had."

"I had the loveliest dream," Brisa replied, rubbing the sleep out of her eyes. "We found a pot of gold at the end of a rainbow. It was *so* pretty."

"Gold, huh?" Sirocco said, smacking his

lips. "That makes me think of honey! I think a little post-nap snack is in order!"

But when the horses arrived in the kitchen, Sumatra was standing between them and their feed buckets. Her eyes glinted with excitement and her back hooves tapped impatiently.

"You're finally up!" she said to her friends. "I hope you had a good rest. You're going to need it!"

"For making a honey run?" Sirocco said hopefully.

"For finding out what our talents are!" Sumatra declared. "I told you I'd take care of everything, and I have. You just need to come with me. Um, now!"

"*Now?*" Brisa squeaked. "There's not even time to fix my hair?"

"Or get a snack?" Sirocco complained. "Where are we going in such a hurry?"

"You'll see," Sumatra said with a gleam in her eyes.

It was afternoon by the time Sumatra led Kona, Sirocco, and Brisa on a secret flight out of the apple tree house and across the dandelion meadow. They flew into the woods until they were in the forest. Finally, Sumatra headed for a dirt clearing in the center of some tall trees.

"Follow me," she said with excitement in her voice. She dove down to the clearing.

"This," Sumatra announced as she landed, "will be our stage!"

Then she pointed with her nose into the dusky air above them. "Up there are our spot-lights," she said. "It gets dark really early in the forest."

There were fireflies bobbing in the air. The

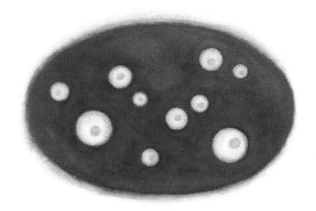

little bugs lit up together, casting a beam of light onto the Wind Dancers.

"Oh!" Kona neighed. As she landed on the clearing-turned-stage, along with Brisa, she squeezed her eyes shut. "Those are bright!"

"Well, they have to be," Sumatra said. "The spotlights have to light up the stars."

"What do you mean?" Sirocco asked. He'd landed on the stage, as well. He glanced upward. "The stars are way up in the sky. And I can't see them, anyway. There are too many tree branches in the way."

"No, Sirocco!" Sumatra explained with

excitement. "*We're* the stars!"

She bowed proudly to her friends with a wave of her front hoof.

"Or rather," she added, "we're *going* to be stars, once we've finished our auditions."

"Auditions?" Kona said. She opened her eyes and squinted through the spotlights at Sumatra. "What do you mean?"

"We'll each do a performance," Sumatra said matter-of-factly. "And then the rest of us will judge our talents. When we figure out what we're good at—you know, dancing, or acting, or whatever—I can start planning our talent show."

"What?!" Sirocco balked.

Kona was alarmed, too.

"We have to perform . . ." she said, looking a little pale behind her violet coat.

". . . right this very minute?" Brisa added, trembling.

22

". . . without any preparation?" Sirocco finished.

"Yeah!" Sumatra said with a gleeful smile. "I promised you an adventure, didn't I? What's more adventurous than a spontaneous performance? C'mon, it'll be fun!"

"Oooh," Sirocco groaned. He clutched at his belly.

"Oh, are you still hungry, Sirocco?" Brisa asked.

"Not anymore," Sirocco said. "I think my butterflies have jumped from my magic halo right into my belly!"

"That's called nerves, Sirocco," Sumatra said with a grin. "But don't worry. Nerves keep you on your toes and can actually make you perform better."

"I should be brilliant, then," Kona said,

23

sticking out her tongue.

Sumatra laughed. Then she added, "The best way to get your hooves wet is to jump right in. Why don't *you* start, Sirocco?"

"Start *what?*" Sirocco said, with panic in his voice. "I don't know what to do."

"Explore your talents!" Sumatra suggested dramatically. "Do whatever moves you. Sing. Dance. Do some stand-up!"

"I *am* standing up," Sirocco responded indignantly. He pointed with his nose at his hooves, which were planted firmly in the dirt of the stage.

"Hee, hee!" Sumatra said. "See? That's funny! Why don't you tell some more jokes?"

"I don't know what you're talking about," Sirocco protested. "I didn't tell a joke in the first place."

"Oh, I guess you don't know about stand-up," Sumatra explained. "You see, it's a kind of comedy."

"Comedy?" Sirocco said, wrinkling his nose at the unfamiliar word. "I thought you said to tell jokes!"

"That's what comedy *is*, telling jokes—oh, never mind!" Sumatra said. "I'll tell you what," she added bossily, "since I'm the director, I'll decide what you should do. Sirocco—sing!"

Sirocco obeyed by crossing his front hooves and taking a deep breath.

"The sun'll come out," he yowled, *"TO-MOR-ROOOOW!"*

"*Eeek!*" Sumatra whispered to herself. Sirocco was screeching the high notes and growling the low ones. There was really not a thing nice Sumatra could say about his song. So, of course, she said nothing at all.

Nothing except, "Okay, I think that's enough . . . Brisa, you're next! Why don't you enter from stage right?"

"Okay," Brisa said brightly. She rose into the air and flew to the left side of the clearing.

"No, no," Sumatra corrected her. "Stage right means to *your* right."

"Oh!" Brisa said with a giggle. She turned her back to Sumatra and wiggled her right front hoof. Then she turned back around and said, "Well, here I am! Stage right!"

"No, not that way!" Sumatra protested. Then she shook her head. "Oh, never mind—forget right and left. Just fly downstage so you're closer to the audience."

"Downstage," Brisa said, thinking hard. "Okay. Here goes."

And she flew down, down, down until she'd landed on the ground. The *dirty* ground.

"Oh, no!" Brisa cried. "I've gotten mud on my lovely hooves! Before I can continue with this audition, I need to get to hair and makeup."

Sumatra tried hard not to roll her eyes. Instead, she called out, "Next!"

But Sumatra was disappointed. So far, both Sirocco and Brisa had not shown a *glimmer* of talent.

But now it's Kona's turn, Sumatra thought to herself. *And Kona's good at everything.*

Kona herself didn't look so sure. She stepped forward, looking serious. Her front legs were stiff and her head was thrust out at an awkward angle.

"*Hey Diddle, Diddle,*" she announced. "By Mother Goose."

"Oh, you're reciting a poem," Sumatra said eagerly. "How impressive!"

"'Hey diddle, diddle, the cat and the fiddle,'" Kona recited, "'the horse jumped over the moon.'"

"The horse?" Sumatra said, cringing. "Um, are you sure that's right?"

"The *cow*, I mean!" Kona corrected herself. "'The *cow* jumped over the moon. The little hog laughed . . .' Or wait—was it a dog? Or a frog?"

"Why not just try the next line," Sumatra suggested gently to her dizzy friend.

Kona nodded.

But when she opened her mouth, no sound came out—other than a weak squeak.

Kona had forgotten her lines.

Sumatra bit her lip and looked at Sirocco helplessly.

"I'll say it for you, Sumatra," Sirocco offered. Then he turned to Kona and yelled, "NEXT!"

Sumatra laughed a bit nervously.

"I guess that's me," she said.

While Kona slunk to the sidelines, Sumatra took a deep breath. She stepped onto the stage. She felt poised. Graceful. *Talented.*

I just hope Kona, Sirocco, and Brisa don't feel bad when they compare their auditions with mine, Sumatra thought to herself.

Then she began to sing.

"The hilllllls are alive, with the sound of muuuuuu-siiiiic . . ."

As she sang, she twirled—around and around and *around.*

Twirling's always a show-stopper, she

thought to herself confidently.

Finally, Sumatra finished her act with a knock-knock joke—a real knee-slapper about an orange and a banana.

Then she took a deep bow and waited for the applause.

But, surprisingly, all she heard was silence! And maybe a groan or two.

"*Owwwwww!*" Sirocco moaned, shaking his head hard. "My ears hurt!"

Meanwhile, Brisa turned to Kona.

"I don't get that joke," she whispered— loudly. "'Orange you glad I didn't say banana?' What does that mean?"

Sumatra frowned in confusion.

"I don't understand," she said. "You didn't like my number?"

Sirocco only shook his sore ears some more. Meanwhile, Kona gulped and hung her tongue out of her mouth.

"All that twirling made me a little dizzy," she rasped. "I think I might throw up."

Sumatra felt a cold chill come over her.

"You hated it," she said to her friends. "You *hated* my performance!"

"Well . . ." Brisa's eyes darted back and

forth, and she looked uncomfortable.

Kona made a woozy sound.

And Sirocco yelled, "What?! I can't hear you over the ringing in my ears."

"I can't believe it," Sumatra wailed. "I've got no talent!"

CHAPTER 3

Gotta Dance

Sadly, Sumatra rose into the air and headed back toward the dandelion meadow. A gloomy Sirocco, Kona, and Brisa followed her. After they'd flown in silence for a while, Sirocco spoke up.

"I'm sorry that you're so *very* untalented, Sumatra," he declared sweetly. "But don't worry. Your show will go on. After all, *my* singing was awesome."

"And my Mother Goose recital was very dramatic," Kona noted, "once I got the lines right."

"And I think I've finally got the stage directions straight," Brisa piped up. "Plus, I have a great idea for how to do up my mane for our show!"

The three Wind Dancers looked at Sumatra expectantly.

But Sumatra only cringed.

And squirmed.

And avoided all six of her friends' eyes.

Sirocco's face fell.

"Oh, I get it," he said sadly. "If you don't have anything nice to say, don't say anything at all, right?"

Sumatra sighed.

"Right," she said. "I guess we're *all* kind of untalented."

"Well, *I* have something nice to say," Brisa responded. "I thought Sumatra's twirling was lovely. She looked like a silver and green top! She didn't make *me* dizzy at all."

"Thanks, Brisa," Sumatra said. "That makes me feel a *little* bet—"

Sumatra stopped herself with a gasp.

"Hey, hold on just a minute!" she said. "Twirling!"

"Huh?" her friends asked.

Sumatra did a neat pirouette in the air.

"Twirling!" she repeated. "And leaping and somersaulting and loop-de-looping!"

"Do you think the audition got to her?" Sirocco muttered to Kona and Brisa. "She's talking crazy!"

"I'm talking *dancing*," Sumatra retorted. "So we can't act. Or sing. Or tell jokes. *Or* tell stage right from stage left. Who cares?"

"*I* care," Kona said with a sniff.

"You've forgotten who we are," Sumatra insisted with another pretty pirouette. "We're the Wind *Dancers*. Forget about all those other talents—we can put on a ballet! A show that's *nothing* but dance."

Sumatra watched her friends' faces slowly change from sad to stunned. Kona was the first to agree.

"Of course!" she declared. "Great idea, Sumatra! Dancing is something we can *all* do. You know, even big horses dance. Their kind of dance is called *dressage*."

"Dress-*what*?" Sirocco blurted. "What

kind of weird word is that?"

"It's pronounced *dress-AHJ*," Kona said to Sirocco. "And it's not weird. It's French for 'training.'"

"Ooh! French!" Brisa breathed, sounding impressed.

"Dressage is all about graceful trots and canters," Kona explained. "Not to mention beautiful pirouettes."

"It sounds *lovely*," Sumatra said, her heart fluttering with excitement.

"Yeah," Sirocco scoffed. "And, we can do that French stuff one better. Because we can do *dress-AHJ* on *air!* No talent? Ha! I don't *think* so!"

He did his own pirouette in the air.

Well, sort of.

His spin was more of a wobbly thrash. It reminded Sumatra of a caught fish, flopping about on the bank of a river.

But since that wasn't such a nice thought, Sumatra, of course, kept it to herself.

Instead, she decided to think about something nice. *Very* nice. She envisioned herself and her friends dancing before an awestruck audience of frogs, birds, bugs, and big horses. They'd all look glamorous. Their magic halos

would be bright and shiny. She would be draped in ribbons and Brisa in jewels. Kona would be decorated with flowers, and Sirocco would be surrounded by butterflies.

And, they'd all be dancing beautifully, of course.

Even Sirocco. All he needs is a little bit of direction—from me! Sumatra thought confidently.

Sumatra was so excited that she cried, "Let's start rehearsing first thing tomorrow!"

This time, she didn't have to coax her friends. They were as enthusiastic as she was. She also didn't have to struggle for something nice to say. A compliment was on the tip of her tongue.

"We," she declared to her friends, "are going to be *fabulous*!"

. . .

Well, I was partly right, Sumatra sighed to herself early the very next morning. *We are fabulous—fabulously* klutzy!

Sumatra and her friends were hovering over the dandelion meadow. Sumatra had made up a short dance for the horses, just to get them started. But already, their rehearsal was going horribly. Kona, Brisa, and Sirocco kept forgetting the steps. Or they remembered them, but did them wrong. *Or* they did them right, but in the wrong order!

"Okay," Sumatra said to the other Wind Dancers, blowing her forelock out of her eyes. "Let's go through this one more time, shall we? Watch me carefully."

Sumatra performed the dance combination for her friends, narrating as she went.

"You start with a tail wiggle," she explained, swishing her tail back and forth vigorously.

"Then you leap." Sumatra sprang through the air, floating in a perfect arc.

"And spin and kick, and work those jazz hooves," Sumatra ordered excitedly as she twirled, whirled, and shook her hooves.

"And end with a flip," she said, curling into a neat ball and tumbling through the air.

"*Ta-da!*" she said proudly as she finished. "See, it's simple!"

Kona, Sirocco, and Brisa stared at her, open-mouthed.

"Simple for who?" Sirocco squawked. "The Lipizzaner stallions?"

But Kona rose up gently and placed a hoof on Sirocco's back.

"Be positive, Sirocco," she said. "Practice makes perfect, right?"

"Right," Sirocco grumbled. "I guess."

Kona turned to Brisa.

"Right, Brisa?" she prompted.

Brisa was staring wistfully up at the clouds. She jumped when Kona said her name.

"What was that?" she said, startled.

"You *did* watch Sumatra's demonstration, didn't you?" Kona asked, looking worried.

"Oh, of course," Brisa said. Then she glanced back at the clouds. "Well, I might have drifted off for a second there. But don't worry. If I forget a move, I'll just wing it. Why else would we have *wings*, right?"

Brisa fluttered her wings and gave a tinkly little laugh—a laugh that made Sumatra grit her teeth.

You can't wing *it,* she wanted to cry out. *This is choreography. Everybody has to do the same moves! At the same time! And as fabulously as me!!!*

Of course, Sumatra didn't say any of those not-nice things out loud. She only sighed and said, "Let's take it from the top. And five, six, seven, EIGHT—"

No sooner had the Wind Dancers begun their number than Brisa cried out.

"*Ow!*" she said. "Sirocco, your tail wiggled right into my eye."

"Sorry!" Sirocco yelled in mid-leap.

Unfortunately, he forgot to *look* before he leaped.

Crash!

Sirocco had catapulted himself right into the branches of the Wind Dancers' apple tree! He straddled a branch, looking woozy.

"Sirocco!" Kona cried. "Are you all right?"

"Keep dancing without me," Sirocco rasped. "The show must go on!"

So, huffing and puffing, Brisa and Kona moved on to the dreaded spin-kick-jazz-hoof-flip combo.

"Okay, let's see," Brisa said, frowning with concentration. "That's jazz kick—"

She wiggled her back hooves.

"—spinning hooves—"

She flung her front legs out in a big circle. And then, she stopped.

"Um, what was the next step again?" Brisa wondered—just as Kona *flipped* right into her!

"Aaah!" Kona cried when her forehead thunked into Brisa's front legs.

"Oh, yeah!" Brisa said cheerily. "The flip! Thanks for the reminder, Kona."

Brisa did a wobbly flip in mid-air, then

grinned at Sumatra.

"You were right," Brisa said proudly. "That *was* simple."

"Oh, right," Kona said sarcastically, rubbing her head.

"A breeze," Sirocco moaned from the tree branches.

"We all agree then," Brisa said brightly. She turned to Sumatra. "*So,* Miss Director. What's next in our fabulous dance show?"

"What's next, Brisa?" Sumatra asked. "Plan B. As in—let's take a *break*!"

"Yay!" Sirocco cried. He flew out of the tree branches and did a celebratory flip in the air—the first perfect flip he'd completed all day.

Sumatra rolled her eyes, but, as usual, she followed her own if-you-can't-say-anything-nice rule and said nothing at all.

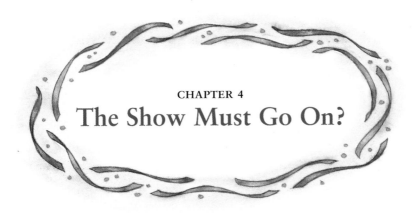

CHAPTER 4
The Show Must Go On?

The next day, as the Wind Dancers stretched their wings and shook out their tails, getting ready for rehearsal, Sumatra gave herself a pep talk:

When Brisa does a flop instead of a flip, she ordered herself in her head, *don't roll your eyes.*

When Sirocco is gangly instead of graceful, don't cringe.

And when Kona slips when she ought to slide, simply smile.

And then I'm going to try something new,

Sumatra thought. *Instead of saying nothing at all, I'll say something nice! That'll boost my friends' confidence! And with more confidence, surely they'll start dancing better.*

Then she clapped her hooves together and said, "Okay, everybody. Let's start off with a simple combination of whirls and twirls, shall we?"

She saw her friends exchange worried glances and giggled to herself.

Wait'll they hear all the nice things I'm going to say to them, she thought.

Only minutes later, Sirocco gave Sumatra her first chance.

"Here goes!" he announced. "Start with a whirl, right?"

He whizzed in a circle.

"Then twirl!" he said, wobbling into a spin in the opposite direction. "Then, whirl, twirl, whirl a-GAIN—*aaaaah!*"

Sirocco had whirled and twirled so wildly that he'd landed right into a tree trunk—a tree trunk that was home to a beehive!

"Oh, no!" Sirocco cried as his *thunk* made honey come pouring out of the hive, right onto his head.

"Why are you upset?" Sumatra said lightly. "You were on a honey hunt when we started this adventure. Now, you've found it. You *love* honey! And look—"

Sumatra pointed at a small swarm of bees that had flown out of the hive to buzz angrily at Sirocco.

"—the bees are annoyed, but they're not stinging."

Sirocco looked at Sumatra suspiciously—while he indeed licked honey off of his nose.

"Yeah, I like honey," he said. "But *you* like perfect dance moves even better. Don't you have any criticism for me?"

Sumatra cocked her head and thought.

"You know, Sirocco," she said admiringly, "I've never seen anyone do dance moves so *fast*! You're not just a whirler. You're a whirl*wind*!"

"Uh, thanks!" Sirocco said with surprise (and another big lick of honey).

Next came a kick sequence—and time for some "nice" words for Kona.

"Whoops!" Kona said as her first kick accidentally connected with an apple hanging from a low tree branch. The apple flew through the air and landed with a plop in a mud puddle near the creek.

"I'll try again," Kona said with a sigh.

Kick! Plop!

This time, Kona's hoof met with an acorn. It, too, sailed through the sky, landing right next to the apple in the puddle.

"Oooh!" Kona growled with frustration. She kicked some more.

Plop! Plop! Plop!

By the time Kona finished practicing her kicks, she was hot and sweaty, and the mud puddle was crowded with two more acorns, one yellow dandelion head, and a mightily disgruntled bluebird!

"I'm awful!" Kona wailed.

"No, you're not. You're a sharpshooter!" Sumatra countered. "Do you realize that every time you kicked something, it landed in exactly the same place? Wow! What aim!"

"O-kay," Kona said. "Whatever you say, Director."

Finally, there was Brisa.

"Try this, Brisa," Sumatra said, doing a tuck and roll through the air.

"Okay!" Brisa said. But instead of a tuck and roll, she did a *roll and tuck*. The jewels in her magic halo made a lovely tinkling sound as she did.

"Um, now how about this?" Sumatra proposed. She lifted her left front leg to do a pretty pirouette, followed by a backflip.

"Sure thing!" Brisa chirped. With a *tinkle, tinkle, tinkle,* she pointed her *right* leg, then did a *front* flip.

"Can you try just a twist?" Sumatra said (with a tiny sigh). She turned to the right.

Tinkle, tinkle.

Brisa turned left.

Sumatra forced a smile and made herself pat Brisa's pretty mane.

"Your jewels sound very pretty when you dance," she offered lamely.

"Thanks!" Brisa said. But then she looked wistful as she gave one of her jewels a *tinkly* tap. Kona and Sirocco were looking a little sad, too.

Oh, no! I don't think my plan is working, Sumatra thought to herself in a panic. *Quick! Say more nice things!*

"You're almost there—all of you," she declared to her friends. "You just need a little more practice is all!"

She waited for her friends to crack a smile, maybe even do an enthusiastic kick or two.

But they only hung their heads.

Desperately, Sumatra tried to think of something—anything—that might make her friends feel good.

"How about taking a break!" she said enthusiastically. "And then we can start working on our big finale!"

"Okay," Brisa, Sirocco, and Kona said dully.

The three Wind Dancers flew to a nearby creek and plunked their sore hooves into the soothing water.

But Sumatra was filled with too much nervous energy to rest.

"I'm going to go over there," she told her friends, pointing at a bit of shade beneath a nearby willow tree. "I'll work on some more

choreography."

Sumatra ducked beneath the wavy willow branches and tried to dream up a fabulous finale for her dance show.

"And a-one, a-two, a one, two, three," she counted to herself as she choreographed her dance. But between the ones, twos, and threes, she was distracted by snatches of her friends' conversation. . . .

"What are we going to do?" Brisa asked Kona and Sirocco. "I'm just not sure we're going to get these dance moves. Sumatra will be so disappointed!"

"And not just Sumatra!" Sirocco complained. "What about the audience? When we mess up all our dance moves, we'll be embarrassed! The snakes will hiss. The porcupines will throw quills. The skunks will make a stink!"

"At least Sumatra's being *nice*," Brisa pointed out. "And she must mean it, because you know Sumatra. If she can't say something nice—"

"—she doesn't say anything at all," Kona

finished. "You're right. And that's why we just have to keep trying. For Sumatra. Putting on this dance show is her dream!"

"I guess you're right," Sirocco said. "Even if we are really sore."

"And tired," Brisa agreed.

"And untalented," Kona said, frowning in disappointment.

"We just have to work harder," Brisa added with a sigh.

Sumatra bit her lip and peeked out at her friends through the leafy willow branches. They were all staring gloomily at their hooves. The flowers in Kona's magic halo were droopy. Brisa's jewels were dull. And Sirocco's butterflies were listless.

Sumatra flew up to sit on one of the top branches of the weeping willow. Honestly, she was feeling sort of weepy herself! She didn't know *what* to do.

If I make my friends keep dancing, she thought, tears gathering in her eyes, *they'll be miserable.*

But if I call the dance show off, Sumatra knew, *then* I'll *be miserable.*

Sumatra sniffed quietly on her bobbing willow branch.

What do I do? she wondered. *I meant all the nice things I said. Sirocco is super-fast. And Kona does have great aim. And Brisa's jewels are very musical. My friends are really fabulous—just not for a dance show!*

Sumatra shook her head sorrowfully and waited for hopelessness to fill her soul.

But instead, she was filled with something else—an idea!

"A *fabulous* idea!" Sumatra breathed to herself. "One that's so crazy, it just might work!"

She burst out of the willow tree with an excited rustle. Her friends looked her way with heavy-lidded eyes.

"Aren't *you* a happy horsey," Kona observed carefully. "Do you have some more complicated new choreography for us?"

"Nope!" Sumatra replied. "Just an announcement. I've decided that we're ready.

The show is going to go on—tomorrow! Let's spend the rest of the afternoon spreading the word through the woods. And then, we'll have our final dress rehearsal."

"What?!" Brisa shrieked. "But we have so much more work to do. Our twirls are terrible!"

"Our pirouettes are awful!" Kona added.

"And our jazz hooves!" Sirocco cried dramatically. "Don't even get me *started*."

"Don't worry, guys," Sumatra declared with a gleam in her eyes. "Leave everything to me!"

"That settles it, then," Sirocco said with wide, scared eyes. "I'm now worried!"

CHAPTER 5
Lights, Camera, Surprise!

By that evening, Kona, Sirocco, and Brisa were *worse* than worried. They were terrified!

The three Wind Dancers were getting ready for the dress rehearsal "backstage"— which was really just an abandoned bird's nest in one of the tall forest trees. Brisa had made mirrors out of magical jewels and propped them on the twiggy walls of the nest. Several fireflies were clustered around each mirror to give the Wind Dancers light to see by.

"I feel dizzy," Brisa said as she peered into

her mirror, decorating her mane and tail with more magic jewels.

"I feel hot, then cold, then hot again," Kona said. She was putting on her stage makeup—berry juice on her lips and black wood-ash around her eyes.

"I think I'm going to throw up!" Sirocco said. The magic butterflies in his halo were looking a little green, too. "Maybe I shouldn't have eaten so many apple muffins at lunch."

Suddenly, Sumatra flew into the nest to join her friends. She was all ready, wearing a dramatic headdress of bright rainbow-colored ribbons and *lots* of berry juice lipstick.

"It's not your lunch, Sirocco," she

informed the colt. "What you're feeling is stage fright. It's completely normal before a big show, even if we won't have an audience until tomorrow. But guess what? I'm going to tell you something that's going to take *all* your worries away."

"Nobody's coming?!" Sirocco cried excitedly. "The show's off?"

"Oh, no," Sumatra said happily. "Everybody's excited about it. The squirrels have already said they want all the balcony seats—"

"Balcony?" Kona said. "What balcony?"

"The tree branches!" Sumatra replied, pointing at the tall trees that surrounded the dirt stage. "And lots of other bugs, birds, and animals are coming, too."

Sirocco's face fell.

"Well, then," he said to Sumatra queasily, "I *really* don't think you can say anything to make me feel better."

Kona and Brisa looked just as gloomy.

"How about this?" Sumatra replied with a sly gleam in her eye. "I have an idea. An idea that changes everything . . ."

· · ·

And that's how the Wind Dancers found themselves—*happily*—in their bird's nest dressing room again on performance day the next evening.

Just as they had the day before, they all decorated their manes and tails with jewels, flowers, ribbons, and butterflies.

But one thing was different from the day before.

The flutters in their bellies? The dry mouths and trembling hooves? All of those things had disappeared.

As Sumatra put the finishing touches on her ribbon-y costume, she peered out of the bird's nest to the stage below.

"The audience is packed!" she reported to her friends. "It's standing room only! Well, standing and flying and clinging to tree trunks, that is!"

"Bring it on!" Sirocco cried.

"You're not nervous anymore?" Sumatra asked him.

"Why be nervous," Sirocco said with a grin, "when you've got talent like mine?"

Sumatra grinned.

"Let's gather for a good-luck nose nuzzle, you guys," she called to the group. All four

Wind Dancers scurried to the center of the nest and touched noses.

"Ooh, I can't wait!" Brisa said.

"Good," Sumatra announced. "It's show-time!"

·   ·   ·

A moment later, Sumatra flew out over the audience, her ribbons trailing behind her. Paws, hooves, and antennae clapped together as she introduced herself and got ready to begin her performance.

This is it! she thought to herself. *My big show has begun. I only wish Leanna could see me now!*

And then, Sumatra began to dance. Her number was full of challenging moves—twirls and whirls, flips and flops, jumps and pirouettes. And lots and lots of jazz hooves.

As Sumatra danced, she could hear the audience *oohing* and *aahing*. They gasped when she dove and sighed when she soared. When Sumatra performed her big finale— complete with lots of big, bold kicks—the animals cheered and shouted.

Sumatra was thrilled as she took her bow.

But it was when she flew offstage that she got *really* excited.

Wait till the crowd sees Kona in action, she thought. She hurried over to the side of the stage, where she'd stashed a feed bucket. The bucket had a hole in the bottom. Sumatra bent her head, put on the bucket, and neighed through the hole. Her voice emerged from the other end, loud and echoing.

"Thank you, thank you!" she boomed through her makeshift megaphone. "For Act Two, we have . . . Kona! Doing a *different* kind of dance."

Proudly, Kona flew out of the nest, looking lovely in her headdress of flowers. From the side of the stage, Sirocco head-butted an acorn toward her.

The audience gasped in confusion—until Kona kicked the acorn with all her might. It shot through the air and landed squarely in a knot in a tree. Right on target.

The audience cheered!

And loudest of all cheered Sumatra.

Sirocco tossed more things, and Kona went after them, all with a big showbiz smile: *kick, kick, kick!*

By the time Kona took her bow, she had punted an apple into Sumatra's feed bucket, a dandelion into the bird's nest dressing room, and a blackberry directly into Sirocco's open mouth.

The crowd went wild!

"I guess I'm not talentless, after all," Kona whispered to Sumatra as she bowed to the audience.

"Nope!" Sumatra declared. "You just had to find *your* talent, Kona!"

Sumatra beamed. Finally, she could say something nice—and really mean it.

Act Three was Sirocco—doing wind

sprints! He circled the stage so fast, he was no more than a blur of golden wings and whizzing butterflies. Then he played a trick, plucking a nut out of a squirrel's paw and planting it into the clutches of a nearby chipmunk so quickly, he could barely be seen.

"Ooh, you better slow down, Sirocco," Sumatra narrated through her megaphone. "The hummingbirds are getting jealous!"

In response, Sirocco grinned and darted upward, flying so high and fast that he poked a hole in a cloud.

The crowd went nuts!

Finally, it was Brisa's turn. She flew out in front of the audience and smiled sweetly.

"I'm going to do a dance, too," she announced. "But mine is a little different."

Brisa began to move. And as she did, she tossed her head.

Her movements hit her halo of gems in such a way that they tinkled out a tune! A lovely, clear *dance* kind of tune.

A deer was the first one to start moving to the pretty music, tapping one hoof in the dirt.

Next, a beaver began thumping his tail on the grass in time with the deer's tap.

A chipmunk hopped in place, and several birds jumped into the air, fluttering their wings joyfully.

Sumatra—who was watching Brisa's performance with Kona and Sirocco—gasped.

"Everybody's having such a good time," she realized, "they're dancing!"

"Well then," Kona said, smiling at Sumatra crookedly. "I guess you got your dance show after all!"

"Except that nobody's pirouetting or dressaging," Sirocco pointed out, with mischief in his voice. "And, ooh, look at that cardinal. He's whirling when he ought to be twirling!"

"And the rabbits are hipping when they should be hopping!" Kona added. "And that deer's jazz hooves are atrocious!"

"Kona!" Sirocco said with a mock frown. "That wasn't nice. You should have said nothing at all! Or you could have said some-thing *super*-nice. That's what Sumatra would do!"

"Okay, okay, enough teasing!" Sumatra protested with a laugh. "But you know what? You guys are right. Instead of trying so hard to say lots of nice things or *not* say *not*-nice things, I should have just been honest with you. *And* with myself. Then I might have realized sooner that trying to make us all into dance stars *wasn't* going to make us happy."

"Lucky for you," Kona joked, "our *true* talents were too dazzling to be ignored."

"Hey, I'll dance to that!" Sirocco said.

He held out his foreleg to Sumatra. Grinning, Sumatra hooked *her* foreleg around his, and they started whirling wildly through the air together. Kona began jigging on the breeze beside them, while Brisa continued to *tinkle* away on her musical jewels nearby.

"So," Sumatra called to her friends as they danced, "do you forgive me for all I put you through the past few days?"

"How can we not?" Sirocco replied with a shrug and a sly grin. "In the end, we *all* got what we wanted. We *were* fabulous!"

There's No Business
Like Show Business

A few days later, the Wind Dancers found themselves in another backstage dressing room. But this time, they weren't in the forest. They were in Leanna's school.

School desks were cluttered with mirrors, pots of makeup, scripts, and sheet music.

The only things missing were the children! That's because Leanna and her classmates were onstage, putting on their big talent show.

"I still don't get it," Sirocco said as he and the fillies flitted around the room. "Why are we back here in the dressing room instead of in the audience, watching the show?"

"Because," Sumatra declared, "we have a

job to do here. And besides, it doesn't matter if the show is perfect."

"Or if there's a jazz hand out of place," Brisa volunteered.

Suddenly, Sumatra jumped. She could hear the thunder of footsteps and the chatter of excited children.

"Quick!" she urged her friends. "We have to finish!"

The Wind Dancers stopped chatting and began to fly from desk to desk, focused on their task. They finished just as the dressing room door flew open and children spilled into the room.

The horses flew up to a windowsill to watch.

"This is actually like a show! I can't wait to see what happens," Brisa said breathlessly.

"Shhh!" Sumatra said with a smile. "It's about to start."

The horses watched the kids high-five each other and shout out congratulations. Then one girl's voice cried out: "What's this?"

"Look!" Sumatra said, pointing her front hoof. "That was Leanna!"

It was indeed. Leanna was standing in front of her desk, gazing at a beautiful bouquet of wildflowers. A similar bundle of congratulatory flowers lay on every desk in the room.

Leanna's teacher gazed at all the bouquets in surprise. Then she turned to the class.

"A star *should* always be given flowers," she said with a perplexed smile. "I'm just wondering who brought all of you these bouquets."

Everyone looked happy, but bewildered, too, as they scooped up their pretty flowers. But Leanna didn't look puzzled at all.

She gazed up at the window where the

Wind Dancers were perched, almost as if she could see them.

It's the Wind Dancers! she thought to herself, hugging her fragrant bouquet tightly. "I just know it."

Sumatra grinned at her friends.

"I think that's our cue," she said with a wink. "Take a bow, everyone."

Laughing, Brisa, Kona, Sirocco, and Sumatra bowed and blew invisible kisses to the celebrating children. Then they turned and flew out the window.

And as they headed off, they twisted, flipped, and *danced* joyfully through the air.

Here's a sneak preview of *Wind Dancers* Book 4:

Horses' Night Out

CHAPTER 1
Rise and . . . Shine?

In the sleeping stalls of the Wind Dancers' apple tree house, all was quiet.

Well, sort of quiet.

Kona was snoring noisily from beneath her horse blanket.

Brisa was giggling her way through a funny dream.

Sumatra's feet were *tap, tap, tapping* on her stall's wooden floor as she dreamed she was dancing in the air.

And Sirocco's stomach was growling. *Loudly.*

"Mmmm," Sirocco murmured in his sleep, his closed eyes smiling. "A second helping of shoofly pie? Don't mind if I do. I hate flies, but I love pie!"

As Sirocco bit into the pie in his dream, his *actual* teeth began *click, clack, clicking.*

His lips smacked wetly.

And he swallowed with great, big *galumphs*, even though all he was really swallowing was air.

"Yum!" said the sleeping horse.

Of course, in real life, Sirocco's belly was still empty. His stomach was *so* noisy, in fact, that it woke him up!

Continue the magical adventures with Breyer's

Wind Dancers

Let your imagination fly!

Sumatra

Sirocco

Kona

Brisa

Collect them all!

For horse fun that never ends!